characters created by

lauren child

YOU
can be my
friend

Grosset & Dunlap

Text based on the script written by Carol Noble
Illustrations from the TV animation
produced by Tiger Aspect

GROSSET & DUNLAP
Published by the Penguin Group
Penguin Group (USA) Inc., 375 Hudson Street, New York, New York 10014, USA
Penguin Group (Canada), 90 Eglinton Avenue East, Suite 700, Toronto, Ontario M4P 2Y3, Canada
(a division of Pearson Penguin Canada Inc.)
Penguin Books Ltd., 80 Strand, London WC2R 0RL, England
Penguin Group Ireland, 25 St. Stephen's Green, Dublin 2, Ireland
(a division of Penguin Books Ltd.)
Penguin Group (Australia), 250 Camberwell Road, Camberwell, Victoria 3124, Australia
(a division of Pearson Australia Group Pty. Ltd.)
Penguin Books India Pvt. Ltd., 11 Community Centre, Panchsheel Park, New Delhi—110 017, India
Penguin Group (NZ), 67 Apollo Drive, Rosedale, North Shore 0745, Auckland, New Zealand
(a division of Pearson New Zealand Ltd.)
Penguin Books (South Africa) (Pty.) Ltd., 24 Sturdee Avenue,
Rosebank, Johannesburg 2196, South Africa

Penguin Books Ltd., Registered Offices: 80 Strand, London WC2R 0RL, England

Library of Congress Cataloging-in-Publication Data is available.

ISBN 978-0-448-44840-4   10 9 8 7 6 5 4 3

I have this little sister, Lola.
She is small and very funny.
Today Lola is excited because
Marv is coming over and he is
bringing his little brother, Morten.

Lola says,
"Me and Morten
    are going to do
LOTS of things together,
    like have a tea party!

I LOVE having tea parties.
    And dressing up!
Everyone LOVES
        dressing up."

Then I say,
        "If you run out
    of things to do,
Morten really likes playing
    Round and Round."

But Lola says,
        "Oh no!
I really do not like
        Round and Round.

All you do is
        go round
and round . . .
        and round.
Nothing happens, Charlie."

Then the doorbell rings
        and Lola shouts,
"MORTEN'S HERE!"

Lola says,
   "Hello, Morten."

Morten doesn't
   say anything.

So Marv says,
   "Morten's not really
a big talker."

And Lola says,
   "Morten, do you want
to see my room?"

But Morten still
   doesn't say anything.

Lola says,
     "Would you like
a **Cup** of **tea**, Morten?"

Morten just stares.

     So then she asks,
"Would you like a **Cookie**?"

Not a peep from Morten.

     "Oh," says Lola.
"Well, what we'll
          do now is . . .

"...**dressing** up!
Look at me, Morten.
I'm a mermaid.

Morten, you can be
a **pirate**."

But Morten
just stands there.

So Lola says,
"I know!
Let's pretend we live
in **Upside Down**."

Lola says,
"In **Upside Down**,
absolutely everything
is completely

¡umop ǝpᴉsdn

Would you like
a **tea** of **Cup**, Morten?
That's **Upside Down**
for '**Cup** of **tea**'!"

Morten doesn't even move.

So Lola shouts,
"Morten?! Don't you
want to play?"

Morten just shakes his head.

Later Lola whispers,
    "Morten didn't like
any of my **games**, Charlie.
        He didn't even
talk to me."

So I say,
    "Marv told you,
Morten isn't really
        a **big** talker."

Then Lola says,
    "But he didn't even
say one SINGLE word.
        He doesn't **like** me."

Then Lola sighs
        and blows some
bubbles in her pink milk.

And do you know what?
Morten starts giggling.

"Hee hee hee hee hee hee."

Then Morten tries blowing
pink milk bubbles.

Lola and Morten
giggle some more.

Then Lola says,
"I know! I know!
Next let's play bubbles
outside.

Morten, what do you
think it would be like
to be inside a bubble?"

"**Bubbly**," says Morten.

"I looooove
being in a **bubble**,"
says Lola.

And Morten says,
"I love being
in a **bubble**, too."

Later, we all have dinner
        downstairs at Marv
and Morten's flat.
        Lola and Morten
can't stop **giggling** and
        whispering together.

Morten asks,
"Would you like to
        play a game, Lola?
It's called
        Round and **Round!**"

Lola looks unsure
so I say, "Go on, Lola."

And Lola says,
"Okay, Charlie. But only
        because Morten is my
new special **friend**."

Morten says,
"Your turn, Lola! What you do is . . ."
"I know," says Lola. "You go **round**
and **round** and **round** . . .
and **round**."